Super
Baby

by Lynne Benton and
Paul Nicholls

W
FRANKLIN WATTS
LONDON • SYDNEY

Franklin Watts

First published in Great Britain in 2016 by
The Watts Publishing Group

Text © Lynne Benton 2016
Illustrations © Paul Nicholls 2016

Series Editor: Jackie Hamley
Series Advisor: Catherine Glavina
Series Designer: Peter Scoulding

A CIP catalogue record for this book is available
from the British Library.

ISBN 978 1 4451 4570 9 (hbk)
ISBN 978 1 4451 4572 3 (pbk)
ISBN 978 1 4451 4571 6 (library ebook)

Printed in China

FSC
www.fsc.org
MIX
Paper from
responsible sources
FSC® C104740

Franklin Watts
An imprint of
Hachette Children's Group
Part of The Watts Publishing Group
Carmelite House
50 Victoria Embankment
London EC4Y 0DZ

An Hachette UK company.
www.hachette.co.uk

www.franklinwatts.co.uk

Mum was asleep in the deckchair. Baby Marsha was asleep in her pram. "I'm bored," said Joel.

Suddenly Marsha sat up
and whistled. Joel stared.

Then the pram began to
move. Marsha giggled.
"No!" yelled Joel.

But the pram went faster.
At the gate, Marsha
whistled again.

The gate opened ...

... and the pram whizzed through. Joel raced after it.

"Come back!" yelled Joel.
But the pram kept going.

It whizzed along the High Street. Marsha giggled.

Just then, a man ran out of a shop, holding a bag.

Goldsmiths Fine Jewels

Martha whistled.
The pram turned and
trapped the man.

As Joel reached the pram, the shopkeeper ran out.

The shopkeeper rang the police. Then he grabbed the man and took the bag.

The police said, "Well done, boy!"

"It wasn't me," said Joel.
"It was my baby sister."

They looked at Marsha in the pram.

"I don't think so," they said.

Joel pushed the pram home. He was puzzled.

"Babies can't whistle, and they can't drive prams," he said. "I must have dreamt it."

Marsha didn't move.

At home, Mum said, "Thank you for taking Marsha out. One day, she'll be big enough to play with you."

"One day," said Joel.
And Marsha winked.

29

Puzzle 1

Put these pictures in the correct order.
Now tell the story in your own words.
Can you think of a different ending?

delighted   fed up

glum

excited   thrilled

annoyed

Choose the words which best describe
Joel and which best describe Marsha
in the pictures. Can you think of any more?

Answers

Puzzle 1

The correct order is:

1f, 2e, 3a, 4d, 5c, 6b

Puzzle 2

Joel   The correct words are fed up, glum.

The incorrect word is delighted.

Marsha   The correct words are excited, thrilled.

The incorrect word is annoyed.